GOOSE'S STORY

by Cari Best
Pictures by Holly Meade

Goose's story is true. She came on a Sunday. We could only guess about how she'd hurt her foot. Had she skidded on the ice as she landed? Could it have been a snapping turtle? Or had some leftover fishing line wrapped itself around her foot? Whatever it was, the goose with one foot became our spring and then our summer that year. Who would have thought she'd become our inspiration for all times, too.

MELANIE KROUPA BOOKS
FARRAR, STRAUS AND GIROUX ▲ NEW YORK

To WW for all the hours of beauty and truth
—C.B.

Thank you, Goose, for inspiring courage and hope.
Thank you, Cari, for your watchfulness, and for transforming what you saw
into a string of words that warm the heart.
—H.M.

Text copyright © 2002 by Cari Best
Illustrations copyright © 2002 by Holly Meade
All rights reserved
Distributed in Canada by Douglas & McIntyre Ltd.
Color separations by Hong Kong Scanner Arts
Printed and bound in the United States of America by Berryville Graphics
Designed by Jennifer Browne
First edition, 2002
1 3 5 7 9 10 8 6 4 2

Library of Congress Cataloging-in-Publication Data
Best, Cari.
  Goose's story / by Cari Best ; pictures by Holly Meade.— 1st ed.
    p. cm.
  Summary: A young girl finds a Canada goose with a badly injured foot and looks for
her each day to see how she is doing.
  ISBN 0-374-32750-5
    1. Canada goose—Juvenile fiction. [1. Canada goose—Fiction. 2. Geese—Fiction.
3. Physically handicapped—Fiction.] I. Meade, Holly, ill. II. Title.

PZ10.3.B4565 Go 2002
[E]—dc21
                                                                    2001027285

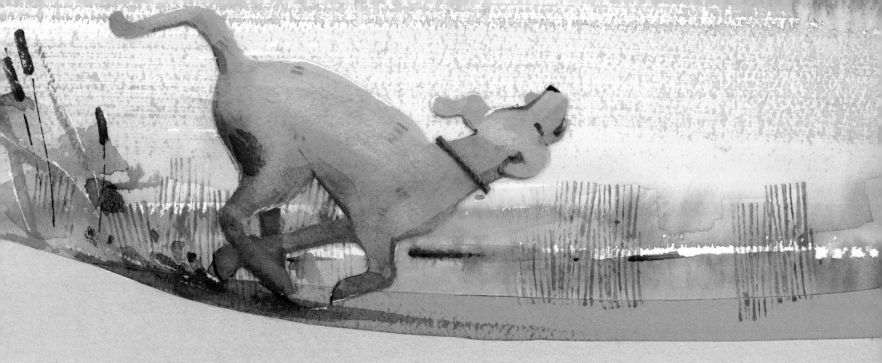

Henry hears the honking first. He circles the pond, around and a half, sending up splashes of warm spring mud all over his winter coat. Henry knows the geese are coming. And then I know it, too.

They land in couples and stand in threes and band together in bunches like people. Old geese, young geese, grandmas, uncles, cousins, and nieces. Each one painted in black and white and gray and brown.

Some geese sit and some geese sleep. Some drink and bathe and swim and sun. Pecking and nibbling, they celebrate spring. All afternoon.

Then Henry breaks free to take back his pond. And the Sunday geese jump for the sky. Their wings spread wider than my arms can reach. Their legs tuck under like airplane wheels. There is honking and barking—and giggles from me.

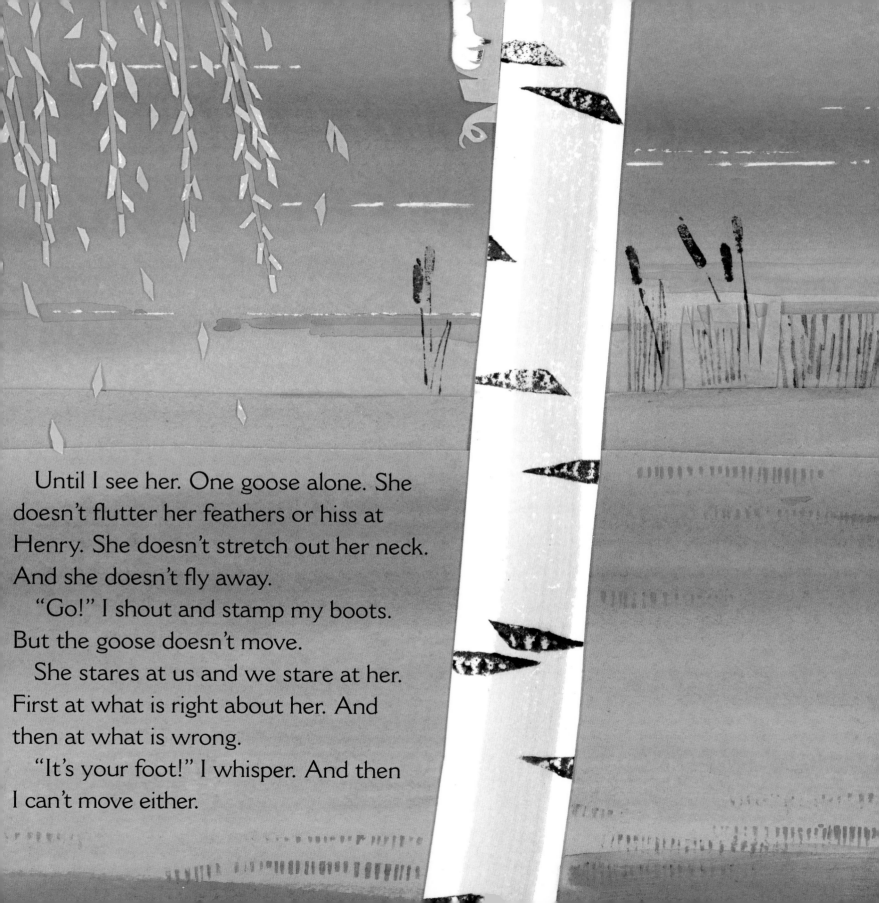

Until I see her. One goose alone. She
doesn't flutter her feathers or hiss at
Henry. She doesn't stretch out her neck.
And she doesn't fly away.

"Go!" I shout and stamp my boots.
But the goose doesn't move.

She stares at us and we stare at her.
First at what is right about her. And
then at what is wrong.

"It's your foot!" I whisper. And then
I can't move either.

My heart is thumping so loud I'm
sure she can hear it. "Oh, goose," I say,
"what happened to you?"

I want to stay and watch her. Make
sure she's all right. But I might scare
her even more. And I'm scared, too.
So I lead Henry toward our house.
To Mama and Papa inside.

The next day when I see the goose, her foot is gone. I feel the saddest I've ever felt. I stand on one foot myself, fixing my eyes on the geese at the other side of the pond. Losing my balance when I've counted to thirty-seven.

"Unlucky goose," says Papa, looking away.

"Some kind of accident," says Mama, looking angry.

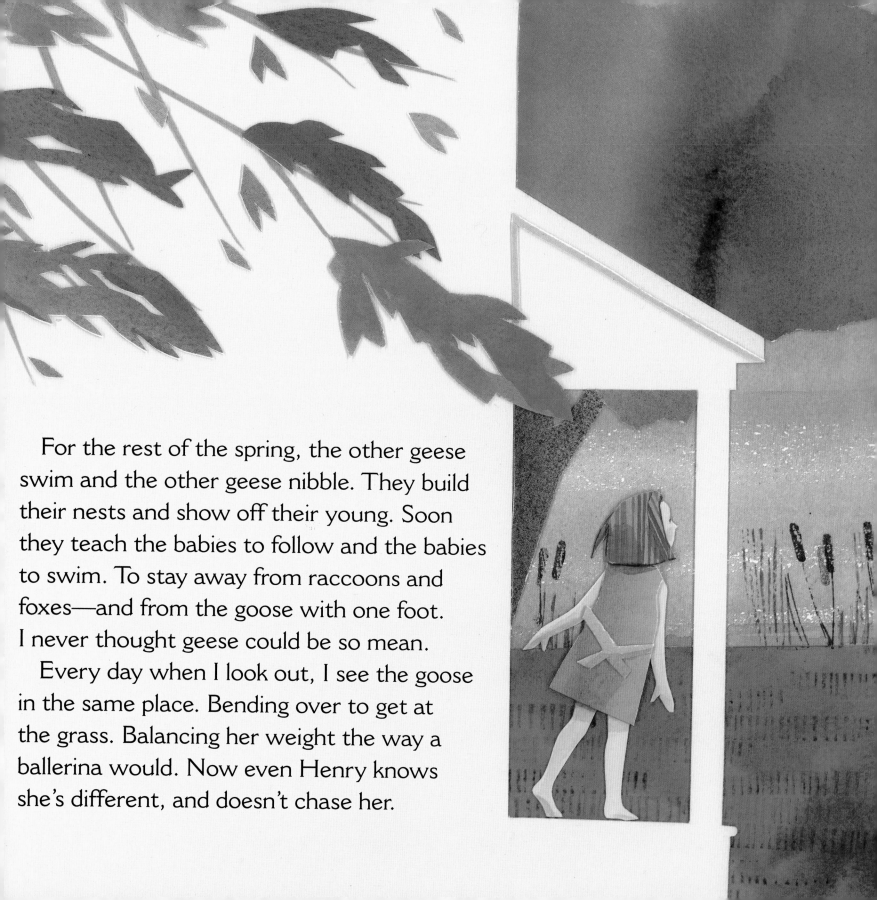

For the rest of the spring, the other geese swim and the other geese nibble. They build their nests and show off their young. Soon they teach the babies to follow and the babies to swim. To stay away from raccoons and foxes—and from the goose with one foot. I never thought geese could be so mean.

Every day when I look out, I see the goose in the same place. Bending over to get at the grass. Balancing her weight the way a ballerina would. Now even Henry knows she's different, and doesn't chase her.

I want to feed her. Pet her. Be her friend.
But Mama says I mustn't. "A wild goose has
to learn to live with her weakness. Or she
won't live at all."

"Try to be strong, little girl," Papa tells me,
"and let her be." But being strong is hard.

When Mama and Papa aren't looking, I sneak my
goose some cracked corn. I talk to her like Mama
talks to me when I'm sick. Soft and quiet. "I'm so
sorry, goose. Does it hurt? Don't be afraid."

Then I tell her a story like Papa tells me before
I go to bed. I blow her a kiss, and whisper, "Try to
be strong, little goose."

One day when I look
out, I don't see the goose
with one foot. I run outside—and
there she is—over where the grass is
greener—hobbling on her stumpy leg.
Like my grandma with her cane.
    "Atta girl," I whisper, the way my teacher
does when I try something hard at school.

The next day I tell her that I'm learning
to swim. "But it's not as hard as learning
to walk is for you," I say. And she listens.
Another day, *she* tries to swim. Slowly
at first. Then faster. Paddling across the
deserted pond. Deserted except for me
and Henry. Cheering.

"If only she would fly," I tell Mama. "Then the other geese wouldn't think she's weak. And she wouldn't always be by herself."

"It's not so easy," Mama says.

"She'd have to push off pretty hard with one foot," Papa tells me.

"Come on, goose," I whisper. "It will be getting cold soon. How will you keep safe when the pond freezes over?"

But she doesn't even try to fly. All summer long, my goose is happy to hobble and nibble and drink and swim.

One day I notice that the other geese have started swimming with her. Hooray! In the water, they look just the same. But I know they aren't.

By September, it's almost time for the geese to fly south. And for me to go back to school. I wonder what will happen to the goose with one foot when the others fly away. I wish she would stay. And I wish she would go. Both at the same time.

"Who will be your friend when I'm at school?" I ask her.

One afternoon when I get home, the geese have gone. I scatter some corn, but no one comes to get it. Henry looks at me, and I look at Henry. We don't know what to think. Except that our goose is gone, too.

For days after, Henry and I hear the trumpeting of the wild geese over our heads. Is our goose up there, too?

We explore every inch of the woods together. Hoping she's hiding. Hoping she's not. We put away the corn till spring. And when the goose music in the sky stops, we give up for good.

All fall and winter, I think about my goose. When I'm riding in the bus, I think I see her. Picking apples, I think I hear her. When I'm playing soccer, I imagine how hard it would be to run with one foot.

In November, I'm in a play at school.

And in December, I get a hamster for Christm

In January, our pond is frozen solid.

And in February, Mama starts her tomato plants indoors.

In March, Henry has begun to shed his winter coat. And Papa says I've grown two inches since summer.

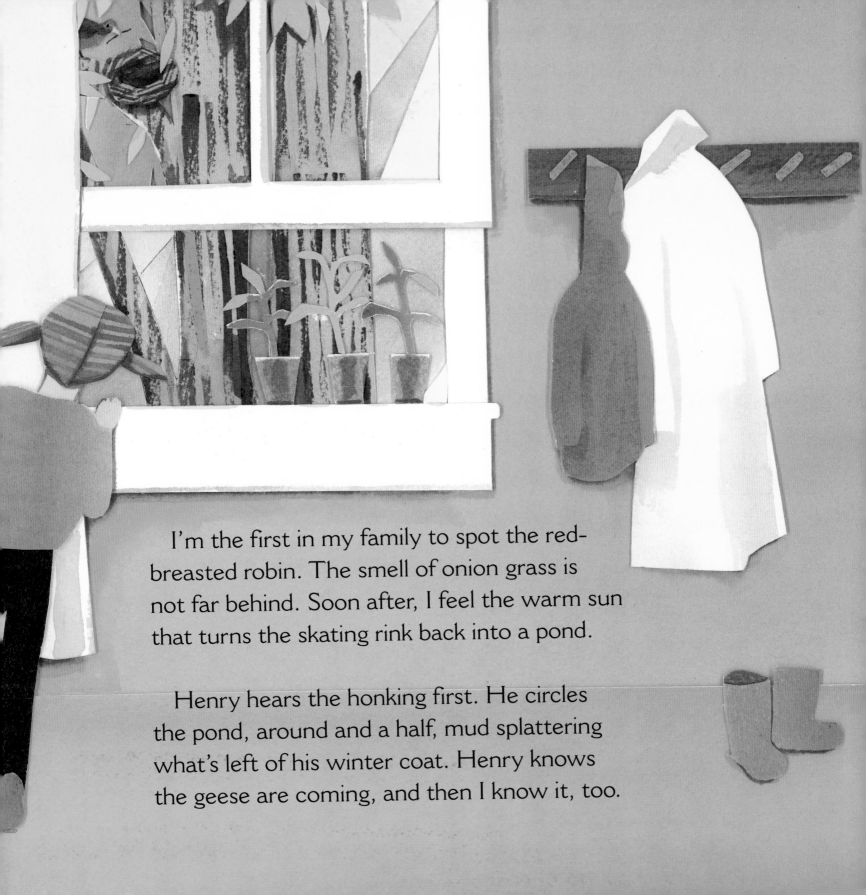

I'm the first in my family to spot the red-breasted robin. The smell of onion grass is not far behind. Soon after, I feel the warm sun that turns the skating rink back into a pond.

Henry hears the honking first. He circles the pond, around and a half, mud splattering what's left of his winter coat. Henry knows the geese are coming, and then I know it, too.

They land together. A couple of geese. Honking and flapping. Drinking and bathing. Combing each other's feathers. One is larger than the other, his neck as thick as a fire hose when he stretches it out to protect her—the goose with one foot.

"It's really you, goose!" I shout. "It's really you!"

For the rest of the spring, two geese swim and two geese sun. Two geese peck and two geese nibble. Side by side, they're always together. Like Henry and me. Friends.

Then one morning in May, I find a big surprise.
There is the goose with one foot and—seven babies!
Seven babies with fourteen feet. Peeping and prancing
and flapping and following. Right behind their papa.
I smile at the parade, and especially at my goose.

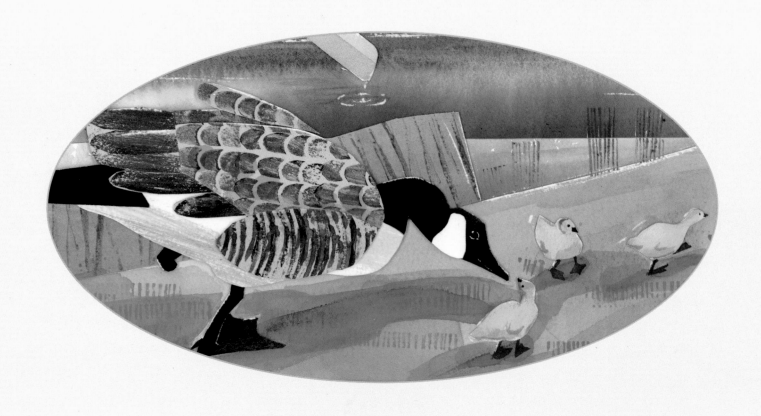

"Look at you," I whisper. "Look at you."